I0762199

ON THE POTTLECOMBE CORNICE

ZEPHYR BOOKS

Classic short works

1. GAUTIER One of Cleopatra's Nights
2. GRAND The Yellow Leaf
3. POWYS The Owl, the Duck, and — Miss Rowe! Miss Rowe!
4. BERRIDGE The Story of Stanley Brent
5. ERTEL A Greedy Peasant
6. RICHARDSON The End of a Childhood
7. POWYS Up and Out
8. MAYOR Miss Browne's Friend
9. STURGIS On the Pottlecombe Cornice

ON THE POTTLECOMBE CORNICE

by

HOWARD STURGIS

Zephyr Books

SANDNESS
MICHAEL WALMER
2022

On the Pottlecombe Cornice first published March 1908
in the *Fortnightly Review*

This edition published 2022

by

Michael Walmer
North House
Melby
Sandness
Shetland ZE2 9PL

ISBN 978-0-6452440-0-7 hardcover

SOME of us who have never ridden in a stage coach, nor had a letter franked by a member of Parliament, who are, in short, in that decent middle of the road of life spoken of by the poet, can yet remember Pottlecombe as a tiny collection of fishermen's huts lying snugly in the bottom of the combe, which took its name from its supposed resemblance to a fruit-basket or pottle. Nothing was easier in passing along the highroad than to miss the rough cart track, which, after climbing a steep hill, descended abruptly to the little fishing village. Those who paused on the crest saw partially-wooded hill-sides slanting steeply on either hand, and in front a V-shaped patch of sea, against which some tuft of flowering gorse, or a great plume of bracken would be sharply outlined in strong contrast of color. Down in the bottom a thin line of smoke would come curling up, or a brown sail flap in the sunlight as a boat put forth to sea.

But the march of progress has invaded even this sequestered spot. A poetess built herself a cottage just above the village, in the height of the then prevailing fashion, with gables and turrets, and no two windows alike. Other villas in the same style as "The Nest" began to crop up here and there on the hillside; the road was widened and improved; a post-office and a shop appeared as though by magic in the village street, and last of all a little crescent of lodging-houses traced its horns upon the slope opposite to the poetess, who uttered shrieks of horror at this profanation of the happy valley. Ten short years had sufficed for all these changes when some local Haussmann conceived the plan of a terrace road, to start just below "The Nest" and wind along the face of the hill towards the sea, following the rise and fall of the coast, and gradually working round to Twistmouth, which all this while had lain within a bare two miles, though more than five remote by the old inland highroad.

The name of the new thoroughfare was the subject of anxious thought with its promoters: "The Parade," "The Marina," "Madeira" were in turn suggested, discussed, and rejected. It was felt by many that the poetess was the proper person to christen this topping achievement of the valley's development; it was known that she was not in entire harmony with the movement, but the fact that no one had made any money by the scheme so reconciled this gifted woman to the innovation, that she ascended the almost finished road the day before its opening, and stood smiling out to sea under her parasol, while attentive friends waited eagerly for her utterance.

"It is beautiful," she said at last. "It reminds me of the Cornice."

The oracle had spoken! The road had received its name, and it added not a little to its impressiveness that most of those who heard it orally had no idea how to spell the word, while those who first met with it in writing were equally ignorant of how it should be spoken.

That a name should be pronounced "Corneechy" and yet written like a plaster moulding, was an idea rich with merriment to the dwellers in the valley and no attention was paid to the complaint of the oldest inhabitant that "there were good enough views and good enough names in Devon to satisfy him without calling it 'Cornish'."

The inhabitants of Pottlecombe found their new road an agreeable promenade for Sunday afternoons; during the week, however, it was apt to lie naked in the sunlight, but for one or two faithful walkers, who took it for their daily beat. Among these none was so constant, in foul weather and fair, as Major Mark Hankisson, a retired military gentleman who occupied the two ground-floor rooms of one of the little houses in the Crescent.

It may be presumed that the Major was not rich; at his age a wealthy man is apt to indulge in the luxury of a body-servant, and to encumber himself with more superfluous accommodation than is to be found in any two rooms in the Crescent at Pottlecombe; on the other hand, if his landlady forgot, in the performance of her various duties, to note the recurrence of quarter-day, the date was unfailingly recalled to her by the neat packet, addressed in tiny handwriting and containing the Major's rent, which she found on the tea-tray when she removed his breakfast things. For all else he paid ready money, subscribed becomingly to the local institutions, and, report said, had ever a little hoard at the call of indigence or distress. A blameless, kindly, contented, gentleman, perhaps a trifle self-centred, yet one whose life was ordered according to the precepts of many admired philosophers. Major Mark (as he was generally called) lay late abed, often not rising before half-past seven—"I am a man of leisure now," he would say, "and may take my rest"; but punctually at ten o'clock he set his aneroid, glanced at the thermometer that hung outside his window, and, carefully dressed, shaved, brushed, stepped forth complete and self-respecting, into such weather as it pleased Providence to send him. On cold days he wore a gray overcoat, double-breasted and cut to the figure, which had grown with years a trifle tight in the waist, and gaped just the least thought in life at the tails. Milder conditions were greeted by a pale dust-colored garment of a kind much worn at race-meetings twenty or twenty-five years ago; this, in the height of summer, was often carried on the arm, or even left at home altogether. Did it rain, the Major was covered to the heels by a black military mackintosh, which flapped around him as he walked, like the wings of a gigantic rook.

His hat was of liver-colored felt, half-high, flat at the top, and tilted rakishly over his nose, disclosing the commencement of his baldness under its hinder rim. He always wore gloves. He walked slowly (no doubt the better to enjoy the prospect) and rather on his toes, the body slightly inclined forward from the waist, the head erect, the chest protruded, the back very hollow.

With many pauses and half-turns, and much "looking before and after," he gained the new Cornice, and followed it through all its sinuosities to the last turn, where it began its descent into

Twistmouth; there he halted and looked down from the heights of a serene contemplation upon the cities of the Plain, for just long enough to enhance his appreciation of the dignified seclusion of Zoar. Then he turned and retraced his steps by the way that he had come, so timing his walk that, with calling at the village post-office for his mail, which consisted almost invariably of the *Standard* of the day before, he reached home just in time to glance over the latest intelligence and assure himself of the death of any old friends before his luncheon, which he took at one o'clock, reserving the leading articles and the notices of new plays as aids to sleep and digestion in the afternoon. Although Major Mark had not been inside a theatre for years, he always read the dramatic criticism with a pleasant sense of being a man about town; he disapproved of "problem plays," and despised variety shows. For Ibsen he entertained a genial and healthy contempt. He liked comedies in three acts, in which beautiful imprudent women in ball dresses who, by innocent indiscretions, had come within measurable distance of injuring their reputations, were saved by cool cynical men with rough tongues and good hearts, in whose place he liked to fancy himself.

Among those who took their exercise upon the Cornice, few, if any, were as regular as the Major, which was no doubt due to his military training. But there was one lady whom, except on the stormiest days, he rarely failed to meet. She was many years his junior, yet by no means in her first youth, and had a little neat, colorless, easily forgotten face. She always wore gray of one shade or another, except when she wore black; but black seemed too positive, too much of a *color,* for her. Her hair was so shot through with white that, had its original hue been darker or more decided, it too would have been gray. A single glance at her would have shown that her careful abstention from feathers was a matter of principle; but sometimes a little tuft of white or lilac artificiality blossomed on her meek hat. She seemed to flutter and run before the wind like a sandpiper, and yet she butted bravely into it when it was against her with force surprising in so frail a creature; but it was on calm days that were yet not bright that the Major thought her most in harmony with her surroundings. That was after he had become aware of her. So unobtrusive was her personality that it was a long time before his mind retained any distinct impression of her as an individual, and even then he thought of her rather as the lady who was always there, than as of a person of any distinctive appearance. Had any strange chance led them both to vary their walk, and so meet anywhere but on the familiar "Cornice," it is doubtful if he would have recognized her.

Day after day and week after week did those two human souls advance, and meet, and pass, and retreat from one another, in this long leisurely country dance, without any thought of becoming acquainted. Probably, in no country but England could such things be. Spring warmed into summer, summer faded into autumn, autumn chilled into winter, and still they saw each other coming up out of the distance, passed dumbly with averted eyes, and did not so much as "speak one another in passing," ere they vanished again over each other's limited horizon.

Sometimes they passed in glorious blue weather, the vault of heaven glowing in a great dome above them, as in Raphael's "Marriage of the Virgin," the sea stretched like another Heaven at their feet, the white road, white sails, and great white flocks of sea-gulls burning and flashing in the sunlight, the air full of the shimmer of heat and the honey sweetness of the gorse. Sometimes the cliffs were red as the heart of a rose, and there were red sails upon the water; sometimes the sea would be streaked with green and purple, the sky would be lowering, and the west wind cry shrilly in the bushes; or all would be gray and very still, save for the soft whistling of the waves as they sucked the pebbles into the broken fringe of foam on the edge of the beach. There were stormy days, too, when the wind seemed like a live thing and tore at the shrieking trees, and the waves arched themselves and fell in thunder, running up among the shingle; at certain corners the rocks stood out into the sea, and here the surf was flung high into the air, almost to the level of the road, and the spray blew wet into Major Mark's face. It was on such a day that he first became aware of a distinct personal interest in the figure of the little gray lady. He hardly remembered so rough a day; the wind took such liberties with the black mackintosh that in the more exposed parts of the road he could scarce make headway. Every now and then he had to turn and let his garment slap smartly down against his calves, while he got his breath, and watched the white shivers run past him on the puddles. Turning to encounter the blast, after one of these breathing pauses, he was conscious of a frail presence blown towards him like a withered leaf by the storm. She was on him, and past, almost before he saw her coming, leaning back on the wind's arm, and beaten out of her usual trim propriety—her decent draperies tightened on her form, her little hat rakishly aslant, a lock of hair broken loose, and even a glimpse of chaste ankles vouchsafed to the public eye. To turn his head and stare after virtuous women on a public road was contrary to the Major's most cherished principles, but for once he was untrue to the tradition of a lifetime, and he always maintained that to know when to be so was the distinguishing mark of a man of action. His mind flew to those corners where the road dipped towards the sea, and where a weak little body sailing on inflated petticoats might be over on the rocks beneath, before the cape could be doubled, unless a stalwart arm were there in case of need. The Major did not hesitate; he brought himself round to the wind, the mackintosh filled, and he started in pursuit. After all it was a free country, and he was on Her Majesty's highway, having an equal right to go east or west. As it was physically impossible for the lady to look round, and all noises were drowned in the roar of the storm and the crash of the waves on the shore, she must necessarily remain in ignorance of his proximity unless circumstances forced him to declare himself; in which case, the service he would render her would be all the excuse he would require. So they sped on, pursuer and pursued, the lady all unconscious that assistance, had she needed it, was so close at her elbow. At each exposed point the Major drew nearer, with extended hand ready to clutch her, at a cry or at any indication that she was being hurried too near the edge; but each time the gray lady steadied herself with unlooked-for powers of resistance, and then shot round the corner into comparative shelter, the Major immediately falling back as soon as the danger was passed.

Three such points of risk lay between the place of their meeting and the final turn of the road inland, into the haven of the combe, and at all three our hero's help was ready, but, as it proved, unnecessary. As the lady successfully turned the last and worst of the three corners, she brought up for a second, gasping, under the lee of the poetess's garden wall. Major Mark stopped himself with an effort from being hurled round on to her, and began painfully to beat up in to the wind again. She was now in safety, and he had no right, no wish, to pry into her further course. Perhaps he was just a little disappointed that his help had not been needed. In the monotony of his daily life, such an occurrence would have been almost an adventure. Even as it was, the thought of what he would have done, how at the critical moment his firm grasp would have averted the catastrophe and steered the fluttering steps to safety, occupied his mind not unpleasantly during the rest of the walk. Once round the corner he would immediately have withdrawn, and, raising his hat, "Madam," he would have said, "it is not safe for you to turn these corners alone: with your permission I will follow near you till we come to the next, when I must beg of you to take my arm." He even took pleasure in thinking out the little speech with which he would have disclaimed her eager gratitude.

By the time he came again to the turn of the road by "The Nest," where he had lost sight of her, the gray lady had disappeared, safely housed, no doubt, from the unsuitable weather into which she had so rashly ventured; nor did the Major see her again for some days. She was by no means as regular in her exercise as he, and after the day in question he found he began to look for her appearance with a certain interest, and to feel that his daily walk lacked something without her. He rallied himself gently on the absurdity of this, but, none the less, it became a sort of game which he played with himself to calculate the chances of her coming, and guess on just which stretch of road they would meet.

The day of the storm had been early in March, and it was not till a hot and breathless July morning in the following summer that the Major accidentally discovered where the gray lady lived. By some chance they had hitherto always met from opposite directions; he had never overtaken, or been overtaken by, her. As he went west he would meet her coming eastward, or if he were returning towards Pottlecombe she would be hurrying in the direction of Twistmouth, and always on the lonelier stretches of the Cornice, away from the houses. It was a very warm day and the lightest of the Major's three overcoats had been left at home; he had even so far departed from the military exactitude of his costume as to take off his gloves.

As he turned the last corner but one on his homeward walk, he observed the object of his interest in the act of rising from the stump of a tree by the roadside where she had been sitting reading a book—the Major felt sure it was poetry. No doubt she had found the day too hot for walking, and so had only brought out her book to a favorite seat from which, when she lifted her eyes from the page, she could look far over the summer sea and let her thoughts wander with the floating gulls. She wore a white muslin blouse, decorated with flat box pleats, down each of which ran a line of neat black herringbone—(though Major Mark's observant eye noted the decoration, he was ignorant of its technical name),—a gray alpaca skirt, and a hat with a small tuft of mauve flowers which the milliner might or might not have intended for Parma violets. Over her head she carried a striped black and white parasol, with a pleasing ogival outline, of a fashion long gone by, which somehow recalled to the Major faint memories of hill stations in India in the early sixties.

Major Mark had had his walk; he was on his way home: the most delicate punctilio did not oblige him to turn in his tracks. Nor, on one of the hottest days of the year, could the strictest code of honor impel him to quicken his pace and pass the lady who had a good fifty yards start of him. It did occur to him with a pleasing thrill that he should in all probability now see where the gray lady lived; but his conscience was white as the dust on his boots; the knowledge would come as the direct gift of Providence and by no act of his.

At the last corner, by "The Nest," the corner round which he had so anxiously watched her on how different a day four months before, the lady paused for a last look out to sea, and he could not repress a hope that she would resume her course before he caught her up; perhaps he even unconsciously walked a little slower. He breathed a sigh of relief; she had gone on, and when the Major rounded the corner, she was some way ahead on the road to the village. Had she, in her glance seaward, become aware of the male figure behind her, and feared that her pause might be construed unmaidenly in her? or did she, perhaps, remember some simple duty awaiting her at home? It is certain that she was hurrying a little.

Just where the road makes its final dip into Pottlecombe, stand a pair of tiny "semi-detached" villakins, rejoicing in the modest names of "Dunrobin" and "Inverary." Into the first of these frail tenements the gray lady disappeared; and the Major noted with pleasure that it was into the house that had the pink standard rose-tree and the white cloves in its front garden. That day when his landlady brought in his frugal luncheon, the Major looked up from the *Standard* and began asking with elaborate indifference who lived in some of the villas on the opposite slope. "And there are two little houses, semi-detached, with turrets at the corners, just at the turn of the road," he said presently, "queer little houses they look. Now I wonder, Mrs. Beer, who might live in those."

"What, they little houses up to the Corneeshy?" she replied to the Major's artless remark, "that look for all the world like the cockle-shell house on my chimney-piece, where the man and woman comes out to tell the weather?"

Major Hankisson admitted the possibility of some such likeness. "There is a pink rosebush in front of one of them," he added diffidently; "do you happen to know who lives there, Mrs. Beer?"

"Eas, a du," assented his landlady. "'Tis Hagsord lives on one, and a wonder 'tis how they gets all their children into the crazy little house. My son Dick, down to the village yonder, he du say the man made his money some kind of chatin' ways, but I tell mun to mind his own business, and not be so gossipy over his na'burs."

"Quite right, quite right, Mrs. Beer," the Major hastened to interrupt. "If we all minded our own business a little more, and were less curious about other people's—" But here he became a little involved, as it occurred to him that his object in the present conversation was not strictly in keeping with the beauty of his sentiments, and, after a most transparently artificial cough, he ended rather lamely: "And who did you say lived in the other house, the one with the rose-tree?"

"The other house," said Mrs. Beer. "Who have I heard lived there, now? Let me see. Aye, the Miss Lambs, it is—maiden ladies, sisters, and much respected. Miss Lamb is some kind of a cripple, bed-ridden, she is, so I've hard; and Miss Agnes, that's the younger sister, she du tend and nurse her. Quiet ladies they be and, as I say, much respected. That keeps theirselves to theirselves; and a wonder 'tis how they can stand the noise of all they childern next door, and one of em an invalid tu."

"Well, I mustn't keep you gossiping all day, Mrs. Beer," said the Major courteously.

"Nor I mustn't stop," hastily assented the landlady. "Plenty have I got tu du, and many things tu attend tu," and her conversation died away down the passage, as a storm rumbles off along a valley. The Major was a very civil gentleman, to the extent of "Good morning, Mrs. Beer, and I hope I see you well this morning," or "Changeable weather, Mrs. Beer, bad for rheumatic people like you and me"; but for him voluntarily to detain her for airy general conversation about the neighborhood, was so unusual an occurrence that Mrs.

Beer being launched on the torrent of much pent-up eloquence had found it difficult to stop.

So now the Major knew the gray lady's name, as well as where she lived. Miss Agnes Lamb; it was a pretty name, meek and gentle, as he was sure she was, as women should be. And she devoted her life to the care of an invalid sister; that, too, was quite in the picture, with the standard rose-tree, and the little green poetry book. He liked to know these things, and to think about them; they made a difference in the interest with which he regarded Miss Lamb when they met on their walks, but if anyone had asked him what it was to him that she nursed a crippled sister, or was in a small way an amateur gardener, he would have found it hard to explain his feeling; to himself he attempted no explanation. To be master of the simple facts of her life made the sight of her more amusing. A wild flower by the roadside becomes an object of more intelligent interest if you know its name and the family to which it belongs. You do not necessarily want to pick it and take it home with you.

Nothing was outwardly changed in the relation of Major Mark Hankisson to Miss Agnes Lamb. They met and passed as heretofore; sometimes the Major wondered if she knew his name, and the place of his abiding, as he now knew hers. He felt a little that otherwise he had an unfair advantage and ought to say to her: "Madam, I know your name and address: mine is Major Hankisson, 3, The Terrace." Had he known a little more about the other sex, he might have been tolerably sure that a lady who gathered every item of news and gossip for the entertainment of a sick sister, as a bird gathers seed and crumbs for its nestlings, would have found out all there was to know about so familiar a figure as himself, long before it occurred to him to make his clumsy inquiries.

While Miss Agnes still fluttered past him, with downcast eyes, and the Major was still dimly wondering as to her knowledge of his identity, a tremendous thing happened. She disappeared bodily. For the first day or two the Major thought nothing of it, but when a week, a fortnight, three weeks passed away without her appearing on the familiar road he began to grow seriously uneasy. It was astonishing how much he missed this little lady, to whom he had never addressed a word. He thought of her waking, he dreamt of her sleeping; her presence had been but a small, if agreeable, incident in his daily round: her absence filled his life. The wonder what had become of her came between him and his food, his sleep, his daily paper. At last he could stand it no longer; and when one day, in passing Dunrobin, he saw a strange lady come out of the door, a tall lady hung over with little bags, and shawls, and lace scarves, and deliberately pull the last pale November rosebud from Miss Agnes's cherished tree, he stepped to the gate, where a fly was standing, and, scarcely knowing what he did, pulled off his hat saying, "Pardon me, madam, the Misses Lamb?" He could say no more, and he never knew what made him say so much, or what in the world he would have done had the strange lady told him they were within, and invited him to enter. She smiled very graciously and said, "The Miss Lambs are away; I have taken their house for the winter"; and, being joined by a maid and a couple of dogs, the whole party got into the fly and rattled off for a drive.

Major Mark did not know at first whether he was relieved or disappointed. They had not gone for good. In the spring she would come again, with the wild-flowers and the swallows. None of the terrible things he had dreamt of had happened to her. She had simply gone away for the winter and let her house. But the winter stretched bare and cheerless before him. He was still four weeks from Christmas, and it was unlikely that the Lambs would return, at the earliest, before May. Five long months must he walk the Cornice alone, and with no hope of seeing the familiar gray figure. The time of waiting must be shortened at any cost. No one knew what had determined the Major to do a thing so contrary to the habit of years, but he actually wrote to a cousin, his nearest surviving relative, and offered to come and pay her a visit.

Mrs. Beer could hardly believe it when he broke the news to her. "Deary me! now, sir, be you really a-goin' away? Well, only to think of it! Keep your rooms? Yes, indeed, and keep 'em safe and clane, and whatever you may chance to lave in 'em, which is more than many could say. And when'll we be looking for you back again, now?"

The Major could not make his absence tally with that of the Miss Lambs. In the first place, to do so might excite remark, and even if his cousins would have kept him five months, he certainly would not have been willing to stay with them for a fifth of that period; so, having astonished them and himself by sojourning in their tents for an uneasy fortnight, having been very kind to the children, and given the one who was his godson ten shillings, he found himself early in January once more in the ground floor at Mrs. Beer's.

Perhaps the family circle of which he had so recently formed an uncomfortable segment made his bachelor life seem a little empty and lonely by comparison. He certainly did not envy his cousin's husband, an anxious, hard-working, careworn man, always fretfully comparing the inadequacy of his means with the ambition of his wishes for his gawky youngsters. Still, the fact remains the Major was not as cheerful, nor as sublimely content and self-satisfied as he used to be; he once even sat down on the stump where

Miss Agnes had read poetry and grew quite tender and sentimental over the thought of his lonely old age, which had formerly never troubled him at all.

Long as was the winter, the spring came at last, with daffodils and primroses; Miss Lamb's namesakes were bleating in the meadows, the west wind blew, and the birds sang late in the long twilights. The Major felt that faint stirring of the pulses, the little return towards our own youth, that comes back to the oldest of us with the youth of the year.

One day, in passing Dunrobin, he witnessed with heartfelt gratification the exodus of the tall lady, with the scarves and shawls and satchels, and the two dogs, mounted guard over by the grim, vigilant little maid. The tenant was gone; then it was not unreasonable to look for the homecoming of the ordinary inhabitants, and sure enough, not two weeks later, on just such a day of veiled radiance as suited her best, one of the many turnings of the Cornice gave the gray lady again to his expectant eyes. He was so glad to see her after her long absence that he forgot the banning want of any official introduction, and making her a grave bow as they met, "Welcome back, ma'am, to the Cornice," he said. "You have been much missed."

Miss Lamb appeared startled, but not displeased, as she bent her head in return to his salutation; a slight color came to her pale cheek, and her lips seemed to speak, though no word reached the Major's ear.

It is curious that it never occurred to Major Mark to try and follow up an acquaintance thus hardily begun. It seemed as if he did not even desire it. Perhaps he felt that mere talk and visiting would destroy the subtle fragrance of this secret silent friendship. It was enough for him that the little lady was back in her accustomed surroundings, and that he should have the mild excitement, as heretofore, of wondering each day if he should meet her, and if so, just where the meeting would be. So another summer wore away, the only difference being that now the Major took off his hat when he encountered Miss Agnes, and made her a fine stately bow, which she acknowledged by a slight inclination and just the faintest tinge of embarrassment at the unusual nature of their intercourse. Sometimes Major Mark would even launch a casual criticism of the weather, as "A fine day, madam," or "Very warm, is it not?" but more commonly they passed in silence as they had done so many times before—as he fully thought they would often do again.

Have we not all passed beside our happiness without recognising it, or, if dimly recognising, yet making no effort to grasp it? Does not the Scripture take the folly of wayfaring men as a fact of universal acceptance?

The winter after that in which the Miss Lambs had let their house, influenza was so rampant in Twistmouth that a stray microbe or two even found their way to Pottlecombe.

"You be careful how you go walking about," Mrs. Beer said to the Major. "Old Fry down to the Blue Swan's got it, and the woman at the post-office, and two of her children, and the minister and all his family; the village is choke full of it. I'm fair frightened to go down to the shop myself."

But Major Mark, going to and fro in the pure air of the Cornice, still set the epidemic at defiance, and noted with pleasure that Miss Lamb appeared to share his immunity.

"Glad to see you've not fallen a victim to the prevalent complaint," he called genially to her one day.

As the autumn changed to winter and the weather grew colder, he had been haunted by a fear that they would go away again, and it was not till Christmas was safely over that he took heart of grace, and refused a rather tepid invitation from his cousin to repeat his visit of the year before.

When, soon after the New Year, Miss Agnes failed to put in an appearance for a week together, he at once connected her absence with this apprehension, and looked anxiously at Dunrobin to see if the house showed any signs of being shut up. On no occasion, however, did lowered blinds give any indication of the absence of inhabitants, and once he thought he could even detect a head which he took to be that of the elder sister in the window of the front ground-floor room.

In spite of these reassuring appearances, a second week had gone before a new anxiety drove the first out of the Major's mind, as one nail knocks out another. Some one spoke of influenza, of its prevalence, of its virulence, of the dangers it left behind it; and behold! something sprang open in the Major's brain with the suddenness of a photographic shutter. How could he have been so dense! If Miss Lamb was missed in familiar places daily, and yet her house stood open to light and life, it was not that she was away, but that she was ill.

As the long weeks slid past, Major Mark found himself going about to try and glean tidings of the little lady in all sorts of hole-and-corner ways, but with scanty success. He would look at Dunrobin blinking with half-drawn blinds at the pale winter sunshine, as though he would force the secret of what was going on within; but those feeble jerry-built walls, with their false air of candor, held curiosity as inexorably at bay as if they had been one of the fortresses which their style of architecture was intended to recall. There was only a little gate to push creaking on its hinges, a step to take, a bell to ring, yet the tidings he longed for seemed as unattainable as if there were moats to swim and frowning bastions to scale at the sword's point.

There comes a moment when suspense grows unendurable, when courage is born of despair, and the thing that has seemed for weeks to be impossible becomes on a sudden the only thing to do, and so simple that we wonder that we have not taken the relief that was being held out to us all the time. One morning, the Major walked straight up from Pottlecombe to the Miss Lambs' door, as if it were the most natural thing in the world, and rang the bell. The summons produced a handmaiden of tender years, with a face like a scared rabbit; but while the Major was still making mincemeat of his first inquiries a thin voice cried, "Show the gentleman in here, Jenny," and he found himself ushered into the front room beside the door. He was confronted by a face, somewhat sharp-featured, and with traces of pain and suffering round the sunken eyes and compressed lips, but not without a certain beauty and dignity. Scanty gray hair was neatly folded round the temples, under a flat scrap of rusty black lace. It was a head of character and strength, but the head alone seemed alive. What was human of the poor little body was kindly veiled under some arrangement of drapery that made it seem one with the couch on which it reposed. "Sit down," said the same sharp little fife-like voice. "You were inquiring for my sister; I am sorry to say she is very ill."

"I must apologize, Miss Lamb," the Major began, "for the liberty I take in calling—"

"Not at all," she interrupted him. "I'm sure it's very kind of you, and I hope you'll come again. I know all about you, and who you are, and it is a comfort to have some one to speak to. I have seen you pass every day for years, and my sister has spoken of you. I am forced to receive you in here; we have no proper sitting-room, so to speak. You see, I have to have this room, because I can't get up-stairs, and I am wheeled into the little back room for meals, but I couldn't sleep there—it's not airy enough; so this has to be bedroom and parlor both for me." It seemed as if the poor lady had been waiting for weeks to talk, and, now that she had got a listener, could not say all she had to say fast enough. The Major began several sentences, but she always stopped him, and went on as if she were saying a lesson.

"Yes—you came to ask after my sister. I know, and it is very kind of you. You may know that we went away last winter: we tried another climate. I am aware that many people thought it was on my account, but it was not. I am as well (or rather as ill) in one place as another. We are not a strong family. My father and mother were both consumptive; but that is neither here nor there. We went for Agnes's—Agnes is my sister—we went for Agnes's lungs: they have always been her weak spot. I think she has injured herself by her devotion to me. I don't deny it." The voice was hard, but the poor eyes were suffused. " I made her go out," she went on almost defiantly, "sometimes I fear when the weather was hardly suitable; still, I felt she ought to go out." The glibness with which it flowed, this explanation that had so much of defence in it, showed how the poor woman had gone over and over it all in her mind on many a sleepless night. It was evidently a relief for once to pour it out to a listener. The vision of the gray lady running before the storm rose on the Major's eye. "But though she had air and exercise," the voice went on, "no doubt it was a life of great confinement; and I suspect, though she won't admit it, that the lifting me in and out of bed was too much for her strength: it is not that I am heavy," with a half-humorous glance downwards at her poor shrunken body, "but I suspect it was too much for her all the same. Last winter she had symptoms I did not like; well—we went away: I think it did her good."

The Major caught sight of the little green volume he had seen Miss Agnes reading on the day when he discovered where she lived: he stretched his hand, and took it from the table very gently, to look at the title; it was a copy of Christina Rossetti's poems.

Miss Lamb followed his movements with a certain bird-like sharpness.

"That is one of my sister's books," she said, "it ought not be down here: she left it the last time—" the voice lost its lesson-like glibness and broke suddenly— "She made herself worse," she wailed. "Perhaps she might not have been so bad, but she got this horrid influenza; she would get up and come down stairs, when she ought to have been in bed, because she knew I could not come up to her; it was all for me: it has always been all for me." With great difficulty she raised a handkerchief to her face and covered her eyes with it.

"My dear madam! My poor dear lady!" the Major said with emotion: he felt he was prying into things very sacred, hidden hitherto from every eye.

Miss Lamb made an effort, but she spoke brokenly. "You have been kind," she said. "You have taken an interest: you can see for yourself what it must be to me to lie here, and think perhaps I have killed her. She is very bad; it has gone to her lungs, and there is pleurisy. And I can't go to her, or nurse her, when she has done so much for me. She lies up there, and I lie down here; only the ceiling between us, but we can't be together. A niece has come to take care of us both; she is very kind, and Jenny is very good, but—but——"

she broke down again and cried silently.

Major Mark had been turning an idea over in his mind, as she talked. He would like to do something for the poor little wreck before him; still more would he like to do something for Miss Agnes. "Could I—" he asked shyly, "would you let me, perhaps, take you up-stairs?"

"Would you? Oh! would you?" cried Miss Lamb eagerly. "I can't tell you how I—how we should *both* bless you."

The Major was, it must be owned, somewhat past his prime, but he was healthy, and had been strong; not without effort, and much bumping of the wall paper, but with infinite precaution to make as little noise as possible, he succeeded in getting the old wheeled chair up from the ground floor to the landing above. Then after a pause, to recover his breath, he redescended, and, lifting the little figure tenderly in his arms, he bore it up-stairs, and set it in the chair, without a word. The niece was summoned and sent in to prepare the invalid. While they waited for her return, Miss Lamb looked at him doubtfully. "Would you—?" she began, and hesitated, "would you like—" but he checked her with a gesture and shook his head. The thought of entering that maiden chamber made his heart thump wildly, but it seemed to him a profanation.

"No—no," he said gently. "I couldn't. You won't misunderstand me, I know. I'll wait out here as long as you like, and take you down again. Don't hurry. I shall like sitting here."

When the chair had disappeared into the sick-room, and the door had closed upon it, he sat down on a little box ottoman draped with meagre chintz, and covered with a white crochet "tidy," that stood under the window. He was very much moved. As he covered his face with his hands, he could feel the hot blood rise in his cheeks under his old palms. He knew now what he had felt for the little gray lady and was blushing like a boy, with a pang that even at that moment was not wholly painful.

When he had got Miss Lamb safely back to her sofa, she detained him a moment as he was leaving.

"Agnes said I was to thank you from *her,*" she said, "and—and to give you her love." He pressed the little crippled lady's hand and went out in silence.

It had been agreed between them that he should return on the following afternoon and repeat the service he had rendered. "Only," Miss Lamb had said, "if the blinds are down, you'll know there is no need."

So when, next day, he came again to the tiny house, a glance at its sheeted windows sent him stumbling along the familiar reaches of the Cornice, where he had been used to meet her, whom now he should meet no more. The west wind moaned softly, in the dead grasses; out at sea the gulls were crying harshly. He seemed to walk in a dream; only, when he came to his usual turning place, he shook himself and looked about him, and then kept straight on down the road into Twistmouth.

There is no church in Pottlecombe; most of the village folk are dissenters and go to the meeting-house. Such of the inhabitants as belong to the Establishment have to trudge two miles or more to a little church on a windy upland, so old that the ground all around has raised its level, and the worshipper steps down in entering to the damp flags of the pavement. Hither, also, whether of the Establishment or not, they must come on their last journey; and it was here that Miss Agnes Lamb was buried on a soft February day like a foretaste of spring. A nephew had come from somewhere and joined the niece, and they two occupied the only carriage that followed the simple hearse; but when the little funeral drew up at the churchyard, Major Mark was there, dressed all in black, and with the very finest wreath he could buy, which he laid on the coffin with something very like a sob.

"Why should Major Mark have gone to Miss Lamb's funeral?" the neighbors asked, "and taken a beautiful great wreath of white flowers from the florist's in Twistmouth; and all in black too, for all the world like a relation? I didn't even know that he knew them. I think he must be going a little touched in his head."

www.ingramcontent.com/pod-product-compliance
Lightning Source LLC
Chambersburg PA
CBHW030612310726
48979CB00003B/672

* 9 7 8 0 6 4 5 2 4 4 0 0 7 *

670_2011737 48979CB3B
5.5x8.5_PS-ING_M
9780645744644

BUMP IN THE NIGHT

Published by Riot Time Entertainment
www.riottime.com.au
ISBN: 978-0-6457446-4-4
Written and Illustrated by P.J Kennan

Follow Riot Time on Instagram

Visit www.riottime.com.au
For more fun kids books

BUMP IN THE NIGHT

What was that?

I was awoken from my slumber
Why I did wonder
For I was soundly sleeping
Eyes shut, I was not peeping
But yes you see it's seeming
That whilst I was dreaming
Maybe even slightly snoring
Still outside the rain was pouring

I was abruptly woken
My peaceful sleep was broken
Not by something that was spoken
Nor by someone that was joking
But by some loud obnoxious THUMP
By something that went BUMP
In the middle of the night
So as to startle and to fright

Now what might it could be
That has startled me
And raised me from my resting
I started with the guessing

My brain it started on a spiral
Of thoughts infected like some viral
Thoughts that turned to be quite vial
Down paths that stretch a mile

What could it be that BUMP
In the night that made me JUMP
Now in my throat a lump
As the blood does start to pump

My eyes still tightly closed
No longer feel composed
The curling of my toes
All adding to my woes
As now I'm heavy breathing
My chest has started heaving
The thoughts that I'm believing
That my mind could be conceiving

Of what could make that noise
And make me lose all poise

Could it be a monster sneaking
And in my room come peeking
For brains that it is seeking
That has got me freaking

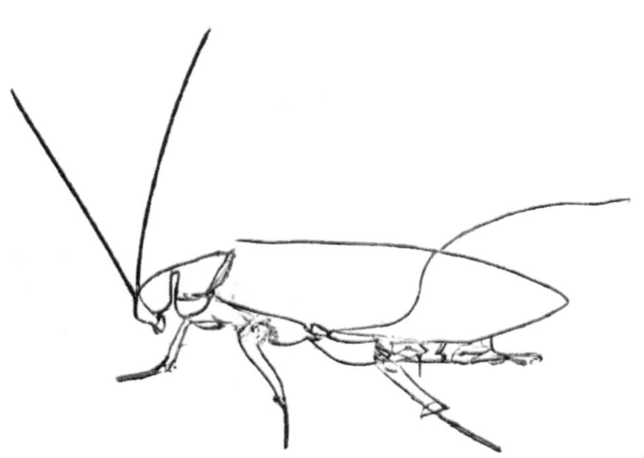

Could it be the roof is leaking
From all the rain that's falling
Or a bug that's crawling
These thoughts are quite appalling

Could it be a dragon growling
Or a witch that's scowling
Or a werewolf howling
Coming to be disembowelling

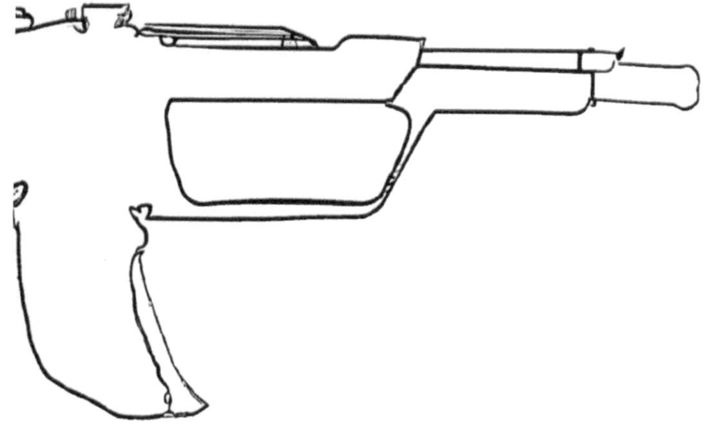

My thoughts now weigh a ton
As imagination starts to run
An assassin with a gun
Into my house has come

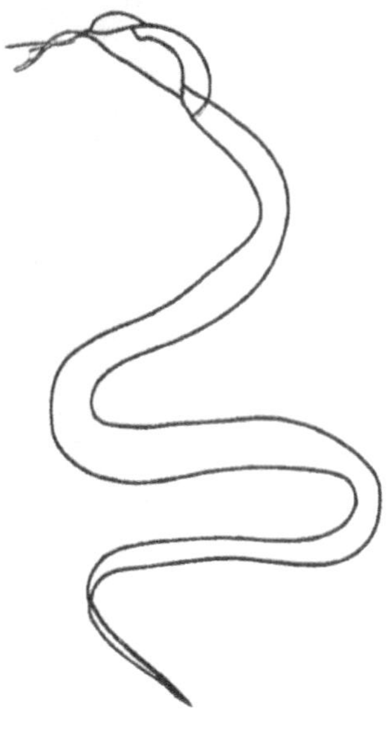

Or a snake that starts to slither
That thought does make me quiver
Like cold I start to shiver
And emotionally I dither

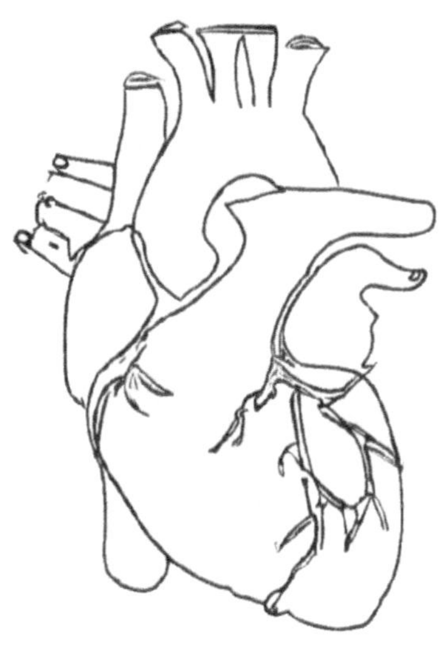

Still darkness does surround
I dare not make a sound
Under covers so not found
My heart does start to pound

Could it be a ghost that's haunting
The thought of it quite daunting
It's wicked ways a flaunting
It's boo that is a taunting

That has wrecked my slumber
I laid there and I wonder
Did I make some blunder
Or was it merely sounds of thunder

This sound
That has made me stir
As I laid there with no one to confer
But my own mind that was a blur

A spy that is a drilling
Camera hole into the ceiling
Or a thief that is stealing
The thoughts have left me reeling

A rat that is a walking
An alien that's stalking
I decided to start talking...

Who's there?

I say so nervous
So soft, could they have heard us?
I must know...
Why have you disturbed us?

With that noise that woke me
From my sleepy peace
That made my deep sleep cease
And caused my heart rate to increase

No answer was forth coming
For a moment thoughts of running
This creature is so cunning
The truth I have been shunning

But still I sat in quite
Deathly silence you should try it
Not a sound that I could hear
No waves upon my ear

As I drifted back toward my dozing
Still stiff like I was frozen
From my fingers to my toes and
No movement I had chosen

I thought I have been but such a fool
The sweat now made a pool
The noise was merely heat and cool
Expansion of the house and some law
of physics rule

As all my thoughts dissipated
Of what possibly had created
That noise that indicated
Something present and had baited

My mind to run so wild
I lay there with a smile
Relaxing for a while
Thoughts discarded to the pile

Feeling somewhat like a chump

Then……

BUMP!

BUMP!

BUMP!

BUMP!

BUMP!

BUMP!

BUMP!

THE END!

www.ingramcontent.com/pod-product-compliance
Lightning Source LLC
Chambersburg PA
CBHW030611310726
48979CB00003B/670

* 9 7 8 0 6 4 5 7 4 4 6 4 4 *